WHAT A SURPRISE

AN ANTHOLOGY OF PROSE AND VERSE

WHAT A SURPRISE

AN ANTHOLOGY OF PROSE AND VERSE

WENDY DEDICOTT
D.P.S.E. M. Coll. T.

ASPECT DESIGN

What A Surprise
Wendy Dedicott

Published by Aspect Design
Malvern, Worcestershire, United Kingdom
November 2009

Designed and Printed by Aspect Design
89 Newtown Road, Malvern, Worcs. WR14 1PD
United Kingdom
Tel: 01684 561567
E-mail: books@aspect-design.net
www.aspect-design.net

A copy of this book has been deposited with the British Library Board

Based on a concept by Wendy Dedicott

50% of the profits from the sale of this book will be donated to UNICEF.

ISBN 978-1-905795-45-1

Dedicated equally to Linda and Frida
and all my friends at South Worcestershire College
for their caring support and friendship.

CONTENTS

ABOUT THE AUTHOR

This is the fifth book from Worcester born Wendy Dedicott. Her previous books are:

Poems of Rural Places (1990)
Cotswold to Celt (1995)
Wild Welsh Wanderings (2003)
Castlemorton (2007)

Wendy has had well over two hundred poems and three short stories published in various anthologies and magazines. In 1999 she received a 'Certificate for Outstanding Achievement in Poetry' from the International Library of Poets and was given the title International Poet of Merit. In 2000 Wendy won first prize in both Papermates Open Competition with her poem 'Light' and in the Westminster Independent Competition with her poem 'Night-time Movement' both of which are included in this book. In 1987 Wendy was awarded an advanced diploma in professional studies in education Dip P.S.E. (CNAA validated as a first degree equivalent), for which she researched into children's creative writing. For some years she also wrote educational book reviews for 'Education Today', the journal of the College of Teachers, of which she is an elected member for this research work and for founding the new concept of 'paired storying', which was used by two English universities and the University of Honolulu!

Apart from writing, Wendy is an enthusiastic painter having begun 'Watercolours for Beginners' at South Worcestershire College (Malvern campus) in 2005. She has also been awarded, by correspondence, London Art College certificates in 'Still Life' and 'Watercolours and Gouache' (with merit).

Wendy is also a keen gardener and has a pond, bog garden and greenhouse and grows most of her own vegetables.

INTRODUCTION

My book contains a varied selection of poems and short stories. Many of the poems were inspired by remote parts of rural mid Wales; some have a religious theme, while others were ideas that were suddenly born in my mind. Some people may have a preference for traditional rhyming verse, which is much easier to write than modern verse. However greater satisfaction is usually received from the creation of modern verse, as it usually has a greater depth of meaning, which hopefully is edifying to the reader. Haiku is a Japanese form of verse.

You may wonder how I decide on a theme on which to write a poem. This may sound strange to you but I don't sit down and wonder what to write about. I am not thinking about writing, then suddenly an idea is born in my mind and the words just come; it's as if I am a secretary for an invisible being in my head. This doesn't happen at a special time or in a special place.

However, the stories were all born following actual events, at which my mother, our dog and I were present.

LIFE WITHOUT END

The ceaseless heartbeat of time
TICKS
on, consigning the minutes to the vast heap of life's
wasted moments, but hark – a distant zooming
motorbike breaks the stillness, perhaps homebound after
NIGHT
club revelry, flashing lights and drum
BEATS
like a mighty
TICKING CLOCK
fulfilling the desire to return to things anticipated.
REGULAR
secure, in the whirlwind of
CEASELESS
change, speed, action, turmoil, but what goal?
Now a droning lorry punctuates the stillness
tortoising along, even the engine exhibits weariness after
CEASELESS
gear changing the
REGULAR
ticking of the indicator like a
TICKING CLOCK
Now the church clock
BEATS
four, consigning another hour to history.
Soon, a new page will turn as
NIGHT
dissolves into day and the metronome of life
TICKS
on.

RUINED MOUNTAIN CHURCH

No doors remain, lights no longer shine forth
Drizzly low cloud shawls each remaining stone.
Strands of sheep's wool hang limply from lichen
My thoughts turn to the weary lead miners
arriving in their hoards, singing praises
with Celtic zeal, invigorated
by the preacher's dramatic pronouncements.
Rustic confetti lies in the corners.
A group of sheep huddle for protection
as birds search the crevices for insects
Within these weatherworn remains there is
an encyclopaedia of knowledge.
Tales of birth and death, heatwave and freeze.
This symbol of faith that radiated
praise across these lonely heights, still remains,
perhaps yearning to tell us the folly
of synthetic values in today's world.

THE SEASONS OF DAY

DAWN, the SPRING of day is born
Fresh
New dew
Cold will unfold
INTO
DAY, the SUMMER of day will display
Speed
Joys, noise
Heat, a treat.
Suns burn, will turn
INTO
EVENING, the AUTUMN of day will bring
Suns
Low glow
Light, less bright
Shade, will soon fade
INTO
NIGHT, the WINTER of day's in sight
Dark
Deep sleep
Rest undressed
REBORN AT DAWN.

SUMMER'S FAREWELL

A red kite ghosts across the rusting moor.
A multitude of swallows swarms skywards.
No passports, no maps, no money, no food.
Guided to their home by an Unseen Force.
The moorland heathers glory is fading
And ochre edged ferns prepare for dormance
Awaiting bluebells resurrection time
Damp slowly rises from the mossy bogs
Where frogs explore and linger pensively
And another Autumn is harvested
As the golden orb slowly sinks downwards
The distant horizon fuses with sky
Soon the lunar searchlight will beam earthwards
In the magical stillness peace will reign.

UPLAND WONDER

Above Pont ar Elan

Oh, how marvellous this all is. In front,
behind, on all sides. I stand and absorb
this living art gallery, this concert
of rural sounds to sustain on dark days.
I'll paint the scene in words, re-create
this perfection. From across distant seas
gentle breezes refresh in Summer heat.
Observe Nature on these crinkled mountains.
Lilliput man, a speck against jagged
peaks. Man's vision perceives surface beauty
and hears Nature's language. Aroma is
another world, identifying birds
and animals, hiding in the sprawling
tangle. Private world, rare glimpses when an
undercover dweller ventures briefly
into our world. Thought, our secret
dimension, hiding in the tangle of
the mind, sometimes daring to venture out
into action. How marvellous this is!

MOORLAND WONDER NEAR GLASLYN

Gliding kites
traverse the sky's changing face
a warm gentle breeze unfolds
across the heather.
No humans disturb
this peaceful scene.
The only sound
a demanding lamb calling
for its mother.

Powerless
we are shawled
in by the natural world.
Words can not express this magnetic peace.
Mountains rise up on all sides,
majestic
rocky, timeless.
Gradually the sun gleams through the cloud
illuminating
a polished silver lake
across the moor.

Man is out of place
insignificant, overwhelmed,
dumb with awe and praise.
In this natural vibrant environment
nature rules omnipotent.

Man is an intruder
in this scene of perfection.

THE LADY OF THE MOUNTAIN

One day we were sitting in my car on desolate high moorland above Newtown (Powys) in October and the mist came down. In the distance a voice was shouting inaudible words and when I stood outside the atmosphere suddenly felt as if invisible people were there. This road was the main stagecoach route from London for many years.

"Help, help," sudden desperate cries penetrated the misty stillness. It was a woman's voice, but Jeremy was unable to locate it on this vast stretch of high moorland.

Hark, there it was again. He listened intently.

"Help, set me free." This time the cries were followed by a weird moan. But who was it, and where did it come from?

Jeremy suddenly felt terror struck. 'Free' from what, he wondered, and why was she so desperate today? Jeremy was alone and he felt uneasy.

Then, out of the gloom, an indistinct shape gradually appeared. Slowly, silently the figure advanced. It was a tall slim lady. Her pace was regular and determined. Jeremy could have moved but he felt compelled to stay. Near a clump of paddling reeds she came to an abrupt halt. She seemed fixed to the spot, as though in a trance. Then, once more, her cries pierced the silence. She was almost hysterical.

She was completely clad in black, her dress and cloak almost reached her ankles. Her pale expressionless face was circumferenced by a black headscarf. Large brown eyes stared through her black rimmed spectacles. She seemed to look through, rather than at things. Suddenly the scene changed.

"The air feels alive as if hundreds of invisible people are encircling us," remarked Jeremy in a quiet, puzzled voice. An invisible blind slowly lowered itself and screened the figure from Jeremy. Suddenly the sound of stagecoach wheels and horses' hooves became dominant. It stopped. Nothing was visible. Jeremy heard footsteps but saw no one. Then the noise of the hooves and the wheels started again, then gradually fused with the atmosphere. Were there now three of them standing there? Jeremy felt so powerless. Slowly the screen began to disperse until it had totally dissolved and the air felt relaxed.

All tension had gone and the lady's stern appearance slowly melted into a smile, then she spoke:

"Go to the old cottage at the bottom of the mountain. Knock on the door and wait."

Then she turned and walked in the direction from which she had come. She behaved like a speaking robot, and appeared to be under the control of a power outside herself. As she went into the distance she mingled into the drizzly murk and finally vanished. Jeremy stood for a moment and pondered … Should he obey her command … why should he? Yet he felt compelled to He felt mystified.

It was a frosty day in late March, yet the cold almost seemed to paralyse the finger joints, although Spring was beginning to reclothe the countryside.

Jeremy recalled passing a shabby cottage. Was this the one she meant? Surely not, but he had passed no other. He remembered thinking how unkempt it looked. He paused and noted the faded identification on the wall 'Henllan' which was barely readable. The curtains hung limp and lifeless at the upper windows, while at the lower windows dull net hung in folds. The brown painted window frames were much in need of renewal. The aged whitewashed walls were discoloured and covered with a thin layer of moss and a rusty drainpipe dangled by the side wall.

As Jeremy walked round the corner the old cottage came into sight. His breath issued forth like steam from a kettle as he paused for a moment. A few more steps and he had reached his destination. But what awaited him now he thought apprehensively.

The unsteady wooden gate was half open as if company was expected. The garden was in a state of neglect, overgrown grass, stinging nettles, thistles. A gnarled apple tree with contorted branches stood in the centre. Jeremy walked through the weedy path and raised his arm to knock. But, to his amazement, the door handle turned silently. The door opened, as if he'd already knocked, yet no one was visible.

"Hello?" Jeremy shouted enquiringly. "Is there anyone there?"

The sound of determined footsteps could be heard approaching. Then a lady appeared … it was the lady he had seen on the mountain! Jeremy recognized her instantly, but her appearance had completely transformed.

"Ah, you came," she said, almost unbelieving.

"Oh yes," Jeremy replied, "but I thought you were expecting me as the gate was already open and the door opened as I was about to knock."

"That's my resident ghost," she said in a relaxed voice, "he always welcomes visitors, you see he used to live here, but more of that later. I'm glad you did as I asked because I have something to tell you."

Jeremy waited eagerly.

The lady was no longer clad in black. The absence of her headscarf revealed long wavy hair. Her long red dress gave her a majestic appearance and her face wore a welcoming smile. She beckoned Jeremy into a brightly lit room and invited him to sit on a green settee. The room was furnished with dark antique furniture and a small harmonium stood in one corner. There was a jug and basin in the middle of the table and a stately grandfather clock faced it. Jeremy looked round with interest. As if to break the silence the lady spoke:

"I feel some explanation is due after the strange events on the mountain. I am 'The Lady of the Mountain' and I was destined to wander the high moorland above Brynglas because of my evil deeds. Now to explain … for many years I lay in wait for travellers, forced their stagecoaches to stop, ordered the occupants out, and while my brother held them down I robbed them. I amassed considerable wealth, but one day I met my match. I heard the rumble of wheels and thought, here's my chance, and it wasn't long before I saw a glow of light struggling to penetrate the mist. When the stagecoach got close I could see that it was large and nothing short of magnificent. A well dressed lady was seated near the window. I strode out into the middle of the road, and shouted 'Halt!' Then I walked purposefully up to the door and ordered the occupant out. Immediately my brother stepped forward and held her tightly but the moment he touched her, he froze to the spot as if glued into position. I grabbed her bag and started rummaging through the contents. But, without warning, I, too, became rigid. I screamed loudly."

"'What is happening to us, what is ha…?' but my voice was halted in mid flow. My brother and I were completely immobilized."

"'Ha, ha,' cackled the lady that I'd robbed. I wanted to look at my haul of money and jewels, but I couldn't."

"'You've lain in wait and robbed innocent people for many years, but now I have been sent to make you mend your ways. I am a witch. I am dressed magnificently to fool you. I am going to punish you for your evil deeds.'"

Jeremy listened in amazement. His feelings of fear had left him, instead he listened with great interest. She continued:

"The witch then raised her arm and changed my clothes into black and announced, 'You will wander the mountains ceaselessly in all seasons for fifty years, one year for each person you have robbed. Then an unknown messenger will free you. Meanwhile your brother will leave the mountain and live in your cottage, but his punishment is to live for ever as an invisible spirit because he planned it all.'"

"Before leaving the witch added that when she had gone we should regain our mobility and that was true," she explained. "It was my brother who opened the gate and the door. For many years I have paced these mountains ceaselessly, always following the same route at the same pace, but now, as promised, the time of my release has come. My punishment ended this morning on the mountain when the veil of guilt lifted from me. Today is the fiftieth anniversary of that unforgettable day."

"Did you hear the stagecoach?" said Jeremy.

"Oh yes," she said, "that was the coach that travelled along here regularly on the way to North Wales. I saw it, although you couldn't. It has passed here daily all those years to torment me. It carries a variety of people over the year, but each year, on the anniversary, the witch travels alone, and as she passes she puts her head through the window and cackles at me. When the coach stopped the witch got out. I saw her, but you couldn't. It was she who had lowered the invisible screen, which radiated that power. I felt terrified as my eyes must have shown. The strong awareness of myriads of invisible people were the many travellers I had robbed over the years."

"But why?" Jeremy enquired.

"They were sent to make me endure a final intense suffering before I was released. They had banded together to show me what it feels like to be powerless. When their power became almost unbearable the screen dispersed."

"Fantastic," said Jeremy, "so it was me who set you free, but why me?"

“You were chosen because you have the ability to hold people’s attention, and I have heard that people far and wide respect you. So you are the messenger that will tell the world what you have seen, and warn them of the danger of cheating people.”

“I will go and warn people; the mission field is all around,” said Jeremy. “I feel honoured.”

Then suddenly she stood very erect, a chill blast filled the room and, with an air of detachment, she spoke in a powerful, commanding voice:

“I am the Lady of the Mountain, the Lady of the Mountain, the Lady…” Her voice echoed into the distance and as it distanced itself she, too, gradually faded away.

Jeremy felt speechless, it all seemed so weird. Now there he was standing alone inside an old derelict cottage. He stepped outside and felt he must get away as quickly as possible. Then he heard the sound of a stagecoach. Just as he imagined it must be passing, it suddenly flashed into view, then disappeared. From the window a lady leaned out and waved – it was the Lady of the Mountain!

INVISIBLE POWER

Standing on the ridge
my body, an obstacle to the gale's urgent journey.
What is its destination?
like Abraham embarking on a journey
not in its own strength.
Clean, powerful, invigorating, whipping my face.
My body filled with God's cleansing Spirit,
evil within exuded.
Turmoil of modern life dissipated
in the majestic power of the invisible traveller.
The Wind of the Spirit, unseen, moving all
contacts into action.
You are here Lord
We can not see You
So close to each of us.
Your Spirit surrounds us
inspiring
as we wonder at the mystery of
Life.

TOO DEEP FOR WORDS

Linguistic symbols jig saw'd into words,
visible echoes of the deepest thoughts
and emotions, but words can not express
the depth of joy I experience in
Your Presence Lord. I kneel and absorb
the wonder of Your deeply moving Peace,
too wonderful to fully comprehend.
O what joy it is to be alone with
You, silently speaking within my heart,
inspiring me with reborn hope, and
fresh courage. Your Spirit breathes within me.
Your Love envelops me. O that I would
recall these precious moments, when life is
hard. Sadly worldly concerns oft consume
good intentions, but You are in the midst
of everything, even when I let
You down. In prayer and meditation we
feed on You, and receive Your Strength. O help
me to remember the agape shown
to me through friends, whom You have sent. Lord, you
are always with me wherever I go,
however I feel. To You O Lord
be praise and glory for Your calming Peace.

THE MOODS OF THE MIRROR

Life taught me
the moods of the lake. To know
from the gigantic mirror
the contents of the meteorological storehouse.
The celestial headlight dominated
the Magdalene blue perfection
from the genesis of day.
As muffling clouds peeped over the mountains
Utopia was destroyed. Uncertainty,
as light played hide and seek, hopping
over ripples, then wearily
moping behind the turbulent grey mass
The Invisible Traveller made its mark
scribbling patterns across the aqua mirror.

Unspoilt youthful dawn is soon
clouded over by tossing waters of
ceaseless change. Unspoken thoughts, the graffiti
of the mind, oft corrode, if not annihilated.

Each morn the mirror portrays a new face
Crying clouds blur the peaceful scene.
When urgent racing clouds jostle, the surface breaks
Perfection is destroyed. Thoughts plunge
down to the depths and
I wait hoping
for signs of peace to re-appear. The
genesis of light will return.

THE RIVER MARTEG IN FLOOD

my **S** terious people high up in the
moun**T**ains have made an excess of drinking
ch**O**colate, because it is
ove**R**flowing and
tu**M**bling

do**W**n between the mountains
fo**A**ming and bouncing over boulders, at a
Tremendous
sp**E**ed, picking up fresh
passenge**R**s from the
bank**S**

It whooshes past, look, there goes a
bra**N**ch, some

pa**P**er, dead leaves, a
b**O**ttle, soon it will join the
Wye, nothing can halt the
fur**Y** of
STORM WATERS IN POWYS

BRITAIN TODAY

Harlequin'd nationalities season our land
So many customs we don't understand
Multi faithed, multi tongued, multi clad, yet the same
Harmonious living should be the aim.
All have different talents which can enrich life
There is no need for racism and strife.
There are disputes and worries, so people get stressed
Stop, look at nature, we are so richly blessed.
The sun shines on all, the countryside's ours
Birds, animals, insects, trees and flowers.
All is needed to make our land whole
Tolerance and friendship should be the goal.

LOOKING DOWN THE TWYMYN VALLEY

Through the damp early morning
BLACKNESS
a powerful glow creeps up
over the mountains shoulder.
An invisible brush sweeps
across the sky, fringing clouds
with amber and soft cerise.
As the Creator prepares
for day the fiery disc
shaves off the last grey misty
wisps revealing the ancient
mountain's bald head. Suddenly
the expectant dawn floods in
glory. The gaunt mountain stands
majestically rigid
THE LIGHT OF THE WORLD
shines on the peaceful mountain
summit, hidden valleys, and
on restless urban chaos.
It does not recognize size,
class or creed. Imperfections
and secrets can not hide. The
Healing Light reveals all.
Absorb this solemn splendour
so that on the darkest days
this vision of perfection
can rekindle hope for this
powerful glow dissolves the
BLACKNESS
that veiled night times landscape.

DON'T LOSE THE POINT

Multi coloured **D**ecorations, brightly lit
L**O**vely, but
What is the con**N**ection with a dimly lit stable?
Great affec**T**ion to mask inequality among colleagues.

Lovely, but often false
What ab**O**ut the true love of Bethlehem?
Many expen**S**ive gifts are exchanged.
Lov**E**ly, but

Wha**T** is the connection with the shepherds
Hundreds copiously feast on luxurious food.
Lov**E**ly, but

What about the **P**oor stable?
Money spent, **O**utings to pantomimes and shows
Indulgence
Do**N**'t forget why Jesus was born
Don'**T** lose the point of Christmas.

LIGHT

The sun moves slowly down the
sky heralding the
EXODUS
of day
TRUE LIGHT
disappears. Objects lose their identity
becoming, black lifeless silhouettes
Artificial orange and halogen light
creepily illuminate the darkness, but
this is not
TRUE LIGHT
Real colours are hidden and artificial
appearances are adopted. Only
TRUE LIGHT
reveals things as they are and
illuminates the mind. Artificial values
foolishly magnetize, but undercover is
REALITY
Depth and character hidden under a mask
of artificiality. All will be revealed when the
GENESIS
of true
LIGHT
returns.

THE WELCOME CANDLE

This story is based on an actual sighting in the Cotswolds while parked in a lay-by near Ebrington above Chipping Campden. Once again on a misty day we saw the glow of a distant light approaching. We looked away for a moment and it had disappeared and we actually saw the gate start to open, then close again! Marshwold I invented from Moreton-in-Marsh and Stow-on-the-Wold.

“Whatever’s that?” whispered Tom mysteriously.

“Look … near the trees, a slowly moving glow.”

Both Tom and his friend Mike stood by the dry stone wall and looked in amazement.

Whatever could it be in such a deserted place with no habitation for miles except ‘The Welcome Candle’ on the limestone ridge.

It was late afternoon. Mist slowly crept over the landscape fusing earth and sky as light began to fade, and rusting bracken stroked the chill air.

As mist shawled in closer, Tom and Mike decided to walk to ‘The Welcome Candle’ and take refreshment.

Meanwhile an owl ghosted across a nearby field. They were intrigued by what they had seen, but decided to keep it to themselves. They entered the deserted pub, ordered drinks and pies and took them to a table by the window.

By now time had buried another day and in the brightly lit room, where they were seated, a large log fire radiated warmth and security. Then suddenly through the dense blackness outside Tom noticed a slowly moving glow approaching. He leant across to Mike and in a loud whisper breathed:

“Look, there it is again.”

The light moved closer to the window and appeared to be suspended, but no person or attachment was visible. The lights in the pub quickly dipped. Then they heard the sound of hooves and wheels close by and the light suddenly disappeared.

Apart from the landlord, who appeared not to notice, no one else was aware of what they had witnessed.

Tom and Mike stayed at the pub overnight and early next morning thanked the landlord for his hospitality, paid their dues and left.

When they stepped outside they noticed hoof prints and wheel ruts a few metres from the window, and curiosity drove them to walk back to where they had seen the light the previous day. But nothing unusual was visible. Crows were searching adjacent fields for food and a stoat scampered into a hole in the limestone wall.

As it was Tuesday Tom and Mike walked on towards Marshwold to explore the many interesting stalls that were usually at the street market.

As they walked they puzzled at the previous day's happenings and decided to return along the same road.

Sure enough there it was again, a slowly moving glow visible through the muffling mist. They stood motionless to see what would happen next. The glow grew brighter as the silhouette creepily emerged to reveal an old man completely clad in black with a deeply folded, expressionless face. He failed to recognize their presence as he walked towards the old wooden gate in the wall.

Who was he? And where had he come from?

Tom and Mike then heard the sound of hooves and wheels once more. They turned to look, but as before, saw nothing, and when they turned back round the man had vanished.

They decided to return to 'The Welcome Candle' and spend a second night there. They sat at the same table and once again the light appeared outside the window. But this time the landlord noticed, and a look of horror clothed his face. As it got nearer it glowed powerfully and the lights in the pub faded until they were finally extinguished, but the room sounded full of voices.

Tom and Mike felt paralysed with fear and wondered what would happen next. They sat motionless and waited. Suddenly the light vanished, the voices silenced, the lights returned and they were left sitting at the table as before. The landlord saw the look of bewilderment on their faces, and beckoned them to the bar. Let me explain, he offered:

"Legend has it that many years ago, when the London stagecoach passed this way, drovers and shepherds often stopped here to rest. It was common knowledge that they often returned from market carrying large sums of money. One evening the stagecoach halted and a robber dashed in, determined to try and steal some money."

"However, the landlord bravely tackled the robber, not knowing that it was a witch. The drover escaped, but in her fury the witch made all the customers disappear and she took the landlord outside, whereupon he, too, immediately became invisible, though he could see others. The witch told him that when he moved away from the pub he would materialize, but if he tried to go back inside he would become invisible again. The drover wanted to show his gratitude to the unfortunate landlord so he searched until he found him at Snowswell quarry. There he thanked him profusely and gave him a lamp that would always light his way and keep him safe. He is occasionally seen wandering along the narrow lanes, but sometimes he comes back towards the pub but when he gets near and tries to look through the window he disappears and only the light remains because it can never be put out, and the witch rides past, grabs him, and takes him back to Snowswell."

"But why did the lights go out and the customers return?" enquired Tom.

"Ah well, rumour has it that the light he holds is very special. His light is the Light of Truth and Reality that removes the mask of artificiality and shows everything in its true colours."

"Although evil made the landlord suffer, he was rewarded for care of his neighbour by receiving a light that would never go out."

At that moment the light suddenly appeared at the window for the third time. Its powerful glow was almost unbearable. Hooves and wheels were heard, but the invisible landlord immediately turned and shone the powerful light at the coach. Momentarily it lit up and both the witch and stagecoach vanished in a puff of smoke.

The landlord re-entered the crowded room and took over at the bar and Tom and Mike were never seen again.

REALITY

Mysterious mountains shawled in mist
Hid the values of Life
A harlequin of green
Had draped the whole scene
But thoughts could no longer climb.
The mind was still and calm
The winds of confusion had ceased
Branches, like contorted arms, no longer mimed.
The mountains were bleak, colourless and silent.
Slowly, shapes like ghosts appeared through the veil.
Ideas that had fought for space dispersed
The mists slowly danced to and fro
Revealing moments of perfection
Finally the mask disappeared
Revealing stark reality.

NIGHT TIME MOVEMENT

SILENCE
A spider
CREEPS
slowly through his web site.
A coach
SAUNTERS
grumpily up the road.
A car
GLIDES
gently past, homeward bound.
A tracksuited athlete
RUNS
along the path panting.
A police patrol car
SILVERSTONES
along, criminal bound.
A fox
RUNS
across the sports field.
An aeroplane
GLIDES
through the blackness, blinking.
A tramp
SAUNTERS
scuffing along the road.
A woodlouse
CREEPS
across the carpet, then
SILENCE

THE AUTUMN STORM

Natures angry
ROAR
ceased and calmness was restored as
BLACKNESS
slowly dissolved into light. The
glowing orb in the sky crept gently upwards from
BEHIND
a deep pink aura. The
VICIOUS STORM
now, but a memory. Lightening had
DEVASTATED
the rustic scene. Life for many had now been
TORN APART
Huge trunks lay at strange angles on the ground.
Other victims leant on survivors for support.
Contorted arms clasped neighbours. Others were
BROKEN
or dangled limply. Perfection had been
DESTROYED
so quickly and transformed into a lifeless landscape. Man
POWERLESS
unable to restore such destruction looked on in
WONDERMENT
at the tremendous
POWER OF NATURE.

POETRY'S QUEST

Recording many linguistic symbols
jig-saw'd into words, visible echoes
of thoughts and emotions, edifying
the writers and consumers self knowledge
and delving into the meaning of life.
Through many drafts the writer matures
moving forward in the quest for wholeness
The meaning, often not at first received.
But each reading can produce new insights
One verse can outweigh a book of prose. Great
revelations, encased between covers
of a book, illuminating the dark
moments, and ingested to enlighten
and resurrect the Spirit, but will it
kindle your fuse, and set your heart aglow?
Only the dawn of the new Genesis
will show its endurance and Power.

SEPTEMBER EVE

Tall sun dried grasses stroke the gentle air
A kite paraglides high on the thermals
visually exploring for his prey.
Bindweed mazes among the undergrowth
Brittle edged foliage dangles earthwards
toasted by the golden orbs blazing heat.
Gigantic straw reels signal harvest
as time slowly buries another year
As summer fades, a sense of loss invades
Soon the Invisible Traveller will
dash round causing Autumnal confetti
to slalom with Olympic speed between
denuded branches . As the air zeroes
precipitation will magnetize on
arboreal skeletons turning them
into magnificent iced ornaments
But now, peace pervades, as harvest brings the
years work to fulfilment. The Creator
has provided for His Creation. But
what bounty will our harvest yield?

THE SCHIZOPHRENIC TRAVELLER

The skeleton of the ancient timber plant stood
Cold and naked
The vicious Autumn storms had
Ripped off all its clothes
The schizophrenic traveller had
Vigorously discoed between the branches
Heavy rain metamorphosed into hail
And boomeranged off the nude branches.
The temperature zeroed
And balls magnetized onto the bark.
Calmness returned. The skeleton resembled
A gigantic glass ornament and stood
Cold and naked.

ETERNAL LEAF

Low cloud shawls the giant
timber plant. Each baptized
bud breaks forth into new
LIFE
Inexperienced and unspoilt. The
INVISIBLE TRAVELLER
roams among the young leaves, testing their strength.
Plentiful water gives refreshment and
POWER
Leaves tentatively wave to neighbours. The
INVISIBLE TRAVELLER
challenges their loyalty and many
cling to their foundation. Weariness
envelops those bruised by the experience.
Unable to resist the tremendous
POWER
they give up, and break loose, falling
to the ground, and mulchify, giving
LIFE
to others.

THE MYSTERIOUS MINER

We spent many hours exploring the deserted lead mine ruins along the Cwmystwyth valley towards Devils Bridge in Cardiganshire. Odd creaks were occasionally heard as were falling noises especially when windy. However the story is completely fictitious.

"Marvellous," exclaimed Jeremy in amazement as he paused along the mountain track.

"Absolutely marvellous … uplifting … exhilarating."

Jeremy could not find words which adequately expressed his feelings. He wanted to burst forth into song, but such an act was not suited to the peaceful surroundings. So he just stood and absorbed the spectacular panorama, until a pair of curlews broke the silence, calling as they flew overhead. Jeremy walked on a few paces then decided to take rest in the shadow of a large boulder as the sun was so hot. He unhitched his knapsack and sat on the grass. As he poured a drink from his flask he pondered on the privilege of being part of such a beautiful scene.

As he rested he noticed a small piece of rock close by. It sparkled magnificently. He reached forward to pick it up and examine it more closely. Minute quartz crystals glistened from every angle. Expensive jewellery could not have twinkled with greater splendour.

The atmosphere was so warm that Jeremy felt himself becoming drowsy. As he slowly drifted into sleep he began to dream about the rock. He felt sure it was getting bigger. But how could it? But it definitely was. Then a small crack appeared down the centre.

"Good heavens, what's happening? It's getting bigger and bigger and the crack is getting wider and wider."

He looked at it in astonishment. The small piece of rock he had held in his hand was gigantic. The crack had widened so much that Jeremy could now walk through it. He was immediately transported into a thriving mining community. It was dim and noisy, wheels were turning, machines were clanking and grinding. Ropes and pulleys were all on the move and men were busily working. Some containers were full of lead ready to take to the surface. A pungent odour filled the air. It was such a contrast to the scene above. A voice suddenly shouted above the noise.

"You are going to save me."

"What?" shouted Jeremy, "I couldn't hear you properly."

"You're going to save me."

Jeremy was unable to discover who had spoken as they all seemed very busy and unaware of his presence.

Then, suddenly, a distant loud rumbling noise was heard and the earth shuddered. The machinery cracked, broke and fell. Jeremy, normally strong and confident, was shaking with fear.

Men scattered in all directions, like sheep under the flight path of low flying jets. There was a tremendous crash, followed by a deafening shriek, then silence. Dust filled the air. Jeremy stood motionless until it began to settle, revealing a chaotic scene with only one lamp left burning. It lit the figure of an old man who was trapped beneath a heavy wooden pole, with a huge wheel precariously perched above him. Without assistance any rescue attempt would be far too dangerous, even if it were possible. Jeremy carefully picked up the remaining lamp and cautiously made his way towards the man. He bent down beside him and could see that he was still breathing, though unconscious. He realized there was no hope of removing the debris unaided, so he decided he must get help as soon as possible. As he searched for an exit, pieces of wood snapped as he stepped on them. The way seemed endless, then suddenly he came to an abrupt halt. A broken crate attached to ropes blocked his way. But this appeared to be an entrance. He shouted up the shaft, but there was no response. He held the lamp high and could distinguish small metal protrusions that helped to keep the wall intact. With trepidation he put his foot on the lowest one and it felt firm, so he decided he must try and climb up to the surface.

He would need both hands so he searched for a small piece of rope which he passed through the ring on the lamp, secured it and hung it round his neck. As he climbed up he could detect a lighter atmosphere. Both his hands and feet were tired, he felt nervously exhausted, but he had to continue. Finally persistence earned its reward and he was out in fresh air.

"At last," sighed Jeremy, grateful for his safe return to the surface.

Momentarily he perched on a rock. He ran his hands through his hair. It felt full of dust and fragments of debris. Suddenly a short cloth capped man with a rugged complexion and gnarled walking stick appeared. He had obviously walked through the forest.

"You look anxious," he said to Jeremy.

"There's been an accident in the mine. There was a dreadful crash, wheels and pulleys collapsed and came hurtling down in all directions. The men all scattered, except one who I discovered was trapped and he needs help," said Jeremy breathlessly, his voice increasing in rapidity as he spoke.

"Ah well, it's the anniversary," said the man, "and I know who can help you. Trust me. Go into the forest. Explain what's happened. Although you will hear nothing, help will appear."

Jeremy had lingering doubts, but he had no option but to trust the stranger, so he acted immediately. He went into the forest, explained his needs and waited. Then, from deep within the undergrowth, he heard a distant growling noise, terminating in a long hiss. At first, fear gripped him and then he thought of the man's words. He HAD to trust. The growling and hissing soon came closer, the bracken parted and a large dragon appeared. He was dark green with large dark eyes and a wide mouth, which incessantly breathed fire. His tail was long and serrated. He stood and listened as Jeremy recounted what had happened in the mine. Then he ceased growling and hissing, looked Jeremy straight in the eye and bade him follow him. But they passed the entrance and stopped by a huge boulder a few yards farther on. Without any effort the dragon pushed it aside and they went inside the mine. They did not need Jeremy's lamp as the dragon's eyes lit the way. Jeremy followed the dragon to where the injured man lay; yet he had not told him the location. The man was still lying motionless, but the lack of light made it impossible to see the extent of his injuries.

Jeremy did not speak to the man, his mind was on what was going to happen next, and how the man would be rescued. Without hesitation the dragon breathed towards the wheel and his fiery breath burnt through it without harming the man. He breathed heavily and the pole rose from across the man's body.

"Fantastic," said Jeremy.

Then an amazing thing happened … the man sat up, thanked them both, got to his feet apparently uninjured and walked towards the entrance. Jeremy hesitatingly said:

"Are you alright, Sir?"

He didn't reply, but seemed in a hurry to get away.

Jeremy and the dragon followed … and once outside the dragon trotted back into the forest, striding over miniature mountains of moss which camouflaged old tree stumps, then he pushed through the undergrowth and was gone.

Jeremy took one final look at the mine entrance. It looked so black inside. Out here it was marvellous. A gentle breeze blew through the reeds, insects hopped between the grass, and perfume from the pine trees floated across the path.

Suddenly, Jeremy felt something touch his arm. It was a sheep sniffing round him and he realized that he had been asleep for some while, as the sun had moved round and was starting to shine across his face. It was with some relief that he realized that the episode in the mine had been a dream.

Jeremy picked up the small piece of rock once again and put it in his anorak pocket. He felt hungry, walked down the track and crossed the road, making for the pub opposite for refreshment. It was a stone building of ancient origin, and tastefully restored. It looked a quiet establishment where he could rest, refresh himself and try and sort things out. He noted the name across the front wall, 'The Full Moon'. He did not recall having seen a pub called this before. He entered and was warmly greeted by a small cheerful lady.

"Good day, Sir, and what can I get for you?" she enquired.

Jeremy liked her casual friendly manner and ordered a beer and salad. The barmaid put his order on the counter. But before going to a table Jeremy started to recount his experience. The lady showed no surprise saying:

"Legend tells that a hundred and twenty-five years ago today there was a dreadful disaster at the lead mine. No trace was ever found of the many men that had gone down the mine that day, save one man who walked out unharmed, and each year on the anniversary weird things happen in these parts."

Jeremy lifted his tankard and plate from the bar and turned to walk to a table. Much to his amazement, seated at the table opposite was the man who had walked out of the mine unharmed. The man's face was expressionless. Jeremy ignored him and went to a table by the window. A few minutes passed and the barmaid went up to Jeremy and enquired if his meal was to his satisfaction.

"Yes, thank you," said Jeremy. Then, leaning closer to her, so as not to be overheard, he said:

"That man over there is the man who was buried under the debris in the mine."

"Where?" she said questioningly.

Jeremy turned, but the man had disappeared. As he turned back round he heard the sound of wheels and horses' hooves. Then as the sound passed the window, a stagecoach flashed into view, and quickly disappeared. A man looked through the window and waved. It was the miner!

POETRY

Before the first millennium
ancient peoples engaged in the
TIMELESS
craft of painting pictures with words
VISIONS
in the mind, seeking to explore
ideas and the meaning of
LIFE
Linguistic symbols woven into countless words.
The deepest
EMOTIONS
locked away to refresh and
ILLUMINATE
The human camcorder stores memories
which poets sculpture into words.
Both reader and poet feed on
POWERFUL IMAGERY
Rhythmic rhyming poetry exhibits perfection
being synonymous with the rhythm of
LIFE.

TRUE IDENTITY

Dominant brown buds
PERFECTLY FORMED
Their embryo awaiting birth. Scales slowly
unfurl revealing magnolia florets.
UNSPOILT
like a new babe
BORN
into a polluted world. Guarded by soft
foliage this arboreal queen dominates.
Clad in
GLORIOUS MAJESTY
any imperfections are masked. Age worn
conifers debased by the Chestnuts youthful
verdure as she reaches out to
PRAISE HER MAKER
True identity is not revealed
in splendid raiment but in
POWER
to understand the storm.

NEW BEGINNINGS

Dawn, the opening of an unspoilt
page. Light has dispelled dense darkness. All is
revealed. What will fill this vacuum?
Excellence or failure. Triumphs or
sorrows. New hope or despair. True Light is
available, but ineffective if
the switch is not activated. People
live in Light or in the dark confusion
of the shroud of night, groping around for
meaning. Switch on the True Light enabling
this unspoilt page to light up the world.

THE REFLECTING MOON

You shone through the midnight window reflecting the
LIGHT
of a presence greater than yourself.
The Great Creator has provided
the sun giving warmth, energy and
LIGHT
enabling the natural world to
flourish. You do not have warmth and energy.
O, earth satellite you
LIGHT
up the darkness of night teaching us we are useless
without a greater power to sustain us.
Humanity lights up the darkness in the world
when it reflects the power of the Creator.
All Truth will be revealed when the
Genesis of True
LIGHT
returns.

CONTRASTS

Oh, where is love in the harlequin of modern life
in the daily Grand Prix on the motorway?
Where is love in the crowded supermarket aisles
in trolleys stacked to fuel obesity?
Where is love in the racist, the mugger, the rapist,
in the mass walkout, street riot and shooting?
Where is love in road rage, drug dealing and
murder, in kidnapping, stabbing and cruelty?

Parked on a remote mountain road a farmer stopped
and asked if I needed help. That is love.

THE POWERFUL SUN

Heat haze dissolves the horizon into
sky. The frosty clarity of St. Mark's
spire is blurred. The celestial red
fiery disc creeps out, dispersing the
shawling mist round ghostly shapes, ambling in
the fields. Soon a glowing radiance
bedspreads the sky. The misty grey lifts to
reveal the ancient mountains bald head.
The mysterious mask is unveiled
as slowly the sun is reborn flooding
the vast landscape in majestic glory.

THE SOLSTICE MAN

We frequently parked in a forestry clearing below Bwlch y Sarnau, north of Rhayader (Powys). One year, on 21st June, in the field opposite bales of hay were gathered together in a low heap. An old man was standing to one side of them. He began to walk across the field. When he was about half way across we looked away. When we looked to see how far he'd got he'd vanished. Strange, but real and he didn't look the sort to turn into an athlete! And crows were circling overhead.

"He's vanished" shouted Ruth frantically to her friend.

"Who's vanished? There's nobody there only a group of sheep."

"But I saw him, just briefly, but I definitely saw him standing by that post."

They were suddenly aware of a lady nearby, clad in black with a distant expressionless face who had obviously heard their conversation, and responded immediately.

"Oh yes, you definitely saw him. Have you heard of the 'Solstice Man'?"

"No," said Ruth.

"Well, let me explain. Several years ago a lady called Dora was taking her usual short cut along this track to Farmer Isaac with fresh bread, when a large black beast slinkily crept out of the tall grass and positioned itself in the middle of the track baring its teeth. Dora stopped paralysed with fear and screamed inwardly, wondering what the next move would be. Then she suddenly noticed a crow circling above her head. Without warning it flew off. Dora had regularly taken this short cut, but never before had she experienced anything unusual."

"She could see Isaac's cottage a few yards farther on, within a clump of trees and wished he was in the field. Then she suddenly noticed him opposite with his sheep and felt sure he must have seen her, but he completely ignored her. She remained motionless as the animal's fixed stare targeted her. Then she heard distant rumbling wheels and hoped someone would notice her and help. As the sound got closer, much to her astonishment it wasn't a farm cart as she'd supposed, but a stagecoach, which momentarily flashed into view, above which circled a crow. Dora said that a lady clad in black stepped out and seemed aware of the situation.

Then she noticed the crow was once again circling above her head, while the lady looked with an unbroken stare at the beast. Then, as if compelled, the beast slowly closed its mouth and walked back into the tall grass. Dora's fear must have dissolved into relief and gratitude, but when she turned to thank the lady she'd vanished. Feeling puzzled she said she crossed the road and continued towards Isaac's cottage, thinking it was strange that he was nowhere to be seen. When she reached the cottage the door was slightly open so she called to him. The response was approaching footsteps. When the door opened fully it was not Isaac standing there, but the lady whose power had saved her from the beast. Seeing Dora's surprise the lady explained saying:"

"'I am the Spirit of good and evil that lives in everyone and the crows are my messengers. When they see help is needed they find me and lead me to it.'"

"Then Dora enquired where Isaac was and the lady asked if she'd seen sheep being rounded up when she'd come across the field."

"'Yes,' said Dora, 'I was puzzled.'"

"'Well,' said the lady, 'I made Isaac invisible because he ignored you when you needed help. Only the sheep see him and hear his commands. But on the anniversary of that day – 21 June – he is visible for a few seconds and then returns to obscurity for another year. After seven years an opportunity will occur for him to help another stranger and if he responds he will re-appear.'"

"Dora looked amazed and started back home along the track."

"Well that explains why he vanished so quickly," said Ruth to her friend. Then a sudden realization struck her and she turned towards the lady to say…

"Wait a minute you look remarkably like the lady that saved Dora and punished Isaac." But she had completely vanished.

Ruth and her friend wanted to get away quickly, but were so intrigued that they walked across the field and through the clump of trees, but there was no cottage, just a heap of old stones and a low ruined wall. As they stepped over the wall to look around they felt someone invisible quickly brush past them. They hurried back across the field as fast as they could and saw a stagecoach flash into sight and the lady in black stepped in!

A WINTER PHOTO

Sylvan skeletons, mahoganied ferns,
weary rain soaked grass resting beneath
grey anticyclonic skies were mourning
the loss of Summer, but overnight the
whole landscape aged, even the smallest thread
of moss had sprouted white frozen whiskers.
Tall crystallized grasses scattered across the
mountainside resembled miniature glass
chandeliers. Sharp pointed ice spears
hung from glazed rocks. The frozen waterfall
glistened in the tepid Winter sunshine.
The Great Creator had evidenced His
Presence. Everything had been treated
equally, not even the smallest grass
had been overlooked. Complete perfection.

DANDELION

Classified as a weed, but so lovely,
so symbolic, resembling a child's
drawing of the sun. Concentric circles
of slim golden petals reaching from the
heart, increasing in size, radiating
glory. Honeymakers visit daily
gathering priceless nectar for honey.
As its Summer days decline fruition
envelops. Goldfinches tweeze at tiny
parachutes bearing the seed of life. The
Unseen Traveller transports others to
new locations to restart the cycle.
BIRTH, GROWTH, GLORY, DECAY, DEATH
then NEW LIFE
A microcosm of the Christian life.
Continuity – LIFE EVERLASTING.

SNOWFLAKES

Alone in the deep silence of the night
In awe I commune with the Word made flesh
His Peace slowly descends to earth
in each gentle snowflake floating earthwards.
Everything duveted with unblemished
purity. In the stillness of night
God has tangibly descended to earth.

SEARCHING

Looking into myself, my brush
dreams slowly across the paper
Fresh eyes function as the brains jury.
There are many images
Evaluate, make choices
Eliminate the unnecessary.
Let reality shine, express it
communicating feelings that the innermost
being has unveiled.
The first men were artists,
in each, the desire to return to perfection.
Artists, seeking to create thoughts
and emotions in colour, attempting
to create a new world.
Art – a living force.

HAIKU

In the ancient church
the mustiness of damp walls
passive and silent.

and old lamps resting
from long hard work, waiting to
spring into action.

then dimly lighting
the words on the damp pages
gently warmed by breath.

from fervent singing
as the magnolia moon
peeps nosily in.

THE MARKET TRADERS

The idea for this story came to me from seeing something that puzzled me. Weekly we'd park at a picnic spot just off the A44 north of Rhayader called Marteg Bridge and I would walk part way up the mountain with our dog. One week I noticed three sides of several pieces of turf cut, and the cut piece was flapped back over the fixed part. On several succeeding visits other areas nearby had received identical treatment. At the same location there was a very old standing stone. Maybe you will see something that sets your creative mind alight, and a story will be born deep inside the real you.

“Whatever’s happening up there? Look!” said John dramatically as dusk fell, and time buried another day. On the mountainside figures were gradually appearing. At first they were silhouettes, then they slowly took on the shape of cloth capped men in casual clothes, each holding a shovel. John and his friend Alan watched with interest as the men assembled in a group and began to dig up the mountain. But why?

Soon darkness obliterated the view and they drove off towards Llanmarder determined to return the following day to examine the scene. Next morning they arrived at first light and walked up to where the men had been digging. An area of about five square metres had been disturbed and rectangles of turf had been cut on three sides. The remaining side was flapped back untidily. John and Alan determined to return again at dusk. When they arrived, sure enough the previous evening’s happenings were repeated. But what were the men doing, and why did they suddenly appear on the mountain at dusk and dig? As they watched they decided to tell someone local what they had seen. The following morning they called at Llanmarder Post Office and were served by an elderly gentleman. Thinking he seemed a likely person to ask, Alan recounted what he and John had seen.

“Oh, so you’ve seen the people digging?” said the man.

“But what are they doing?” asked Alan.

“Well,” replied the man “Rumour has it that about a hundred years ago an old man called Silas lived in a small stone cottage up on the mountain at Tegmar, where people gathered bilberries in summertime. The railway ran along the side of the mountain en route from Monhar to Dinall. Market traders regularly used the train to travel to market at Dinall. On their return they were often laden with lots of money. Silas knew that Rhys, the farmer, always sold out and regularly got off the train at Tegmar halt.

One October day, when the rusting bracken crouched near the ground, heavy with dew from the enveloping mist, Silas lay in wait for the train's return. Soon he heard it lumbering along. It made its usual stop at Tegmar and, as predicted, out stepped Rhys carrying two large bags. The train slowly moved on and Silas walked towards Rhys. After a short chat Rhys accompanied him to his cottage. But what happened inside nobody ever knew because Rhys never travelled on the market train again, much to the amazement of his fellow traders.

"But why do translucent figures appear on the mountain and dig?" asked Alan.

"Well, after Silas died, his cottage gradually became derelict and collapsed, but nobody ever knew what became of Rhys or the money. A large rock now stands near where Silas is said to have chatted to Rhys. Some say that each October he rises up from the rock and joins the market traders who appear at dusk and dig up the mountain, hoping to find the missing hoard of coins. Some say that when the digging stops and the people disappear Silas materializes, digs up his money and buries it elsewhere, hoping no one will ever find it."

"Ah," said John, "that explains why the turf has been disturbed in so many places."

They then thanked the man and left. Out of curiosity John and Alan returned to Tegmar a week later, and walked up the mountain to examine the area. Much to their astonishment two very old bags lay on the mountainside. But were these the bags that had contained the coins? They never knew because when they bent down to look at them more closely they had completely vanished …

The place names mentioned are derivations of real places:
Tegmar – Marteg
Dinall – Llanidloes
Monhar – St. Harmon
Llanmarder – Llangurig, Marteg, Rhayader